The Crowns and the tales
OF
Apowaaii

VERA ADJIN

The Crowns and the tales
OF
Apowaaii

VERA ADJIN

Books Academy LLC
112 SW H K Dodgen Loop
Temple, Texas 76504
Hotline: (254) 800-1189

Ordering Information:
Quantity sales. Special discounts are available on quantity purchases by corporations, associations, and others. For details, contact the publisher at the address above.

Printed in the United States of America.

ISBN-13:   Paperback   978-1-966567-20-2
               eBook   978-1-966567-21-9

Library of Congress Control Number: 2025900747

Acknowledgment

I also want to thank my life partner, **Kwame Adjin,** and my children **Anastasia, James, Emmanuel, Richard, Christopher,** and **Veronica**, for their endless love and encouragement. I extend my deepest gratitude to the following families and individuals:

The Kwofie family, the Wreh family, the Yankson family, the Ackom family, the Ansanyi family, the Revived Church of God family, the Pobee family, Theresa Bacani, Latanya Frye, Rebecca Aggrey, and all my nieces and nephews.

I also want to send lots of love to my grandchildren, Ernest, E.J., Elianna, Eliora Vera, Serene Paris, Riah, and Daxton. I send great love to my in-laws, my nursing school study partners during my Seton Hall University years, Professor Veronica at Hostos Community College, my godmother Mina Ankrah, and my godchildren Nathaniel Asare, Eva Princess Acheampong, and Joy Fuentes.

I also want to express gratitude to all my co-workers from the past and present. Last but not least, to my childhood friends Cecilia Koomson, Victoria A. Yankson, and Grace Wood. Thank you for your support.

Thank you to pastors and pastoral-related personnel, all the various law enforcement agencies, all Veterans, all health care workers, teachers, journalists, actors, actresses, TKD ladies club members, and the entire Ghanaian community for your existence.

God Bless you, and may you be safe always.

Dedication

To all the hard-working men and women in the world.

And also, to all those that always go out of their way to help other people.

Once upon a time, there lived a princess named Elianna. She was loved by her mother and father very much and all the staff in the palace. Her father used to be a professor until he was summoned to take the throne when his father, the king died of natural causes. Her mother retired as a registered nurse from Saint Veronicas' teaching hospital when Elianna was born and now she is the head of health services for the city. Every evening Elianna and her mother take a walk in the palace garden and after walking around the palace garden for two or three times as their exercise routine, they will take a seat in the multi-flower garden and discuss what was happening around the world, especially in the newspapers in their area.

Elianna was only six years old but had knowledge beyond her years because her parents home-schooled her and gave her open knowledge about everything there was. One day after their normal routine Elianna told her mother that she wanted to stay in the multiflower garden for a few more minutes and her mother agreed.

While she was sitting in the garden alone thinking about how she would rule the kingdom with a kind and caring heart in the distant future because she was the only heir to the throne of Apowaaii, a huge rainbow bird with two heads, one on each end of this bird-like sheep-like creature landed at the front of the seat. At first, Elianna was very afraid and jumped from the seat and hid behind one of the trees in the multi-flower garden. Her heart was racing and she was trembling like a dry leave, as she began to scream the bird said

"Please Princess don't be afraid for I am here to protect you from all the bad things that will befall you in the near future. I will also guide and serve you and be your friend now and forever if you let me."

Elianna was surprised that the birdlike creature could talk. She slowly came out from hiding behind the tree and sat back down on the seat.

"You startled and scared me at the same time. Who are you and where did you come from?" Asked Elianna.

"My name is Leezeek and I come from the great beyond, your fairy mother sent me because you are respectful, obedient, honest, and given to everyone therefore, you have ended the golden star service from your fairy mother who has been taking care and looking after you spiritually from since you were born. And just so you know, no one can see me besides you. However, the only way someone will see me was if I let them." "

"How?" asked Elianna. "

"I can work magic through the sunlight, or the rain drops or the wind or the normal air we breathe."

"Wow that is cool!" said Elianna.

"No that is not all, I can also let you see things through my lens but I have to ask permission from your fairly mother."

"Oh my God! I have a fairy mother, how is she and what does she look like?"

"Am not allowed to say, my orders are to protect, guide, and serve you in my fullest capacity." Answered Leezeek.

"Ok! So what now?" Asked Elianna.

"I will be by your window every night to fly you around and if you don't feel like it, I will just sit and watch over you and guard all the palace on your behalf. Remember you cannot tell anyone about me or what I have told you until further notice."

"Thank you Leezeek see you tonight," said Elianna.

Just as they finished the conversation, Elianna's mother Queen Annabella called her back to the palace. She ran back to the palace and got ready for dinner.

Elianna helped the staff clean and set the table up for dinner even though is not her duty to do that. She continued to the kitchen to assist the staff bring out the desert and the plates. She sat down at the beautiful well decorated oak table and the cook Miss Hanson gave her a piece of chocolate and raspberry pudding.

Princess Elianna was very gracious as always. After dinner, princess Elianna's mother read her a story titled "The Challenge".

The Challenge

Once upon a time, there was a challenge in the animal kingdom that required the fastest animal to be the leader of all the animals in the kingdom. It was an exciting time because all the big animals knew how to run fast and thought they would win and become the leader of the animal kingdom.

On the day of the contest, all the animals were gathered in the animal park with their families, friends, and devotees cheering them on. The contestants were all given numbers, no female animals were included because, in the animal kingdom, only the male animals are allowed to be head of the family. Monkey 1, wildebeest 2, Hippopotamus 3, Zebra 4, Leopard 5, Giraffe 6, Tiger 7, Cheetah 8, Lion 9, and Elephant 10.

It was an exciting time for all in the animal kingdom. The referees were 2 ostriches, 2 flogs and 2 dogs this decision was made and voted on by the grownups of the animal kingdom to ensure that, there are no bias during the contest. The dogs were late because they lived in the city out of the animal kingdom, nevertheless, everything went on smoothly after their arrival.

The contestants will run a quarter mile in the first round, a half mile in the second round, and one mile in the final round. The 2 ostriches will be at the starting point and one will blow the whistle to start the first round, the 2 frogs are to mind the middle sidelines and make sure every contestant stays in the right lane and the 2 dogs will supervise the finish line and make sure to see the right winner.

So, at the first whistle sound, the contest began and it was spectacular, family and devotees were making a lot of noises and you could hear distinct animal sounds from insect sounds to turtle sounds to monkey sounds even the snakes were making funny noises in support of their animal friends. At the end of the first round, the monkey and elephant were disqualified. The elephant which was wearing number 10 was disqualified for not staying in the lane but running outside the lane and the monkey wearing number 1 was also disqualified for not really running but hopping quickly through the first round. Giraffe came last in the time limit the contestants needed to qualify for the second round so he was also out.

So now the rest of the contestants for the second round were: number 3 hippopotamus, number 8 cheetah, number 2 Wildebeest, number 9 lion, number 5 leopard, number 7 tiger, and number 4 zebra.

The cheering continued and the whole animal park was full of dust winds, loud unique noise of talking, and of laughter. The entire park has become celebratory grounds even though the challenge is not finished yet.

At the sound of the second whistle, the challenge became more intense and more serious that even the devotees turned on each other especially the family and friends of the tiger began an intense argument with devotees of the leopard that almost resulted in a fight but the family of zebra stepped in and calmed them down successfully.

At the end of the second round only the lion with the number 9, the cheetah with the number 8, tiger with the number 7 were qualified for the final round. Hippopotamus with number 3 had a heart attack and the wildebeest which is known to be one of the fastest animals among them tripped and fell and was not able to finish the second round. They were carried from the field to a safe place behind the park where the animal emergency clinic was set up.

The family and friends including the devotees of the wildebeest were very sad and some even began to cry but the wildebeest told them, "Hey guys cheer up everything happens for a reason so hold your peace because I am good".

The animal park was on fire literally and it was fun to watch.

So as the hot afternoon sun was about to turn to soft evening sun, the last and final round of the challenge was called with the following animals very eager to finish first and become the leader of the animal kingdom.

Tiger number 7, cheetah number 8, and lion number 9 came back to the start line and the entire animal park went bananas, with screams and animal songs. It was just beautiful to watch. However, a few seconds before the ostrich could blow the final whistle, the entire animal park went extremely silent and you could hear a bone drop and every animal in the park suddenly bow to celebrate the final three contestants.

The respect, honor, and the togetherness they showed were unbelievably stunning.

The final round was intense and quick, the whole one-mile race lasted less than 42 seconds and cheetah number 8 finished first, lion number 9 finished second, and last but not the least was tiger number 7.

After the challenge when the crowning time came this was what Cheetah the winner said to the entire animal kingdom, "My fellow animals, I am honored that you want to crown me the leader of the whole animal kingdom, however, I cannot accept these responsibilities because I am not a responsible and friendly kind. Besides I do not like meetings and community gatherings so effective immediately, I relinquish my position to the lion. We all know that from time immemorial he and his ancestors have been the leaders of this kingdom. So, it will not be right to take the leadership position from him since they have been doing a great job".

And so, the entire animal kingdom accepted the proposal of the cheetah, and the lion was crowned the king of the animal kingdom, and every animal and its kind went back to their corner of the kingdom and they all lived peacefully ever after.

The end.

After the story, Princess Elianna went up, had a bath, and brushed her teeth, and got ready for bed as she does every night, she said her prayers,

"Lord God of everything, watch over me, my family and friends, and the entire world as we go to sleep until the rising bright sun wakes us up peacefully, this I ask in the name of your son Jesus Christ, Amen."

With anticipation and excitement in her heart, she kissed her mother good night and went into her room.

At dawn when the whole palace was quiet and the guards were comfortable in their corners talking about their daily affairs and struggles, Leezeek appeared in Princess Elianna's room.

"Are you ready to go for a ride princess?" Asked Leezeek.

"Yes I am, I have been looking forward to this ride since you told me about it," said Princess Elianna.

"Jump on then," said Leezeek.

Princess Elianna had the time of her life because Leezeek flew over a forest with beautiful mountains, rivers with spectacular waterfalls, and cities with magnificent landscapes and also showed her where the boundaries of her city ends.

It was a night to remember and Princess Elianna was very happy and grateful for the ride. Leezeek returned to the palace after almost three hours of flying over the most adorable and fantastic places in the land. Elianna went to her room safely without the guards seeing or hearing a sound from her. And so, this became princess Elianna's nightly hobby for many years.

One day when Princess Elianna was 10 years old, her mother Queen Annabella went to a medical conference in another city with her three guards and never returned. Princess Elianna was devastated; she cried every day especially when she was in the multiflower garden wondering what had happened to her mother.

Meanwhile, Leezeek has already left to the great beyond for the fairy parents and their assistants' meeting. These types of meetings happen once every ten years and last a whole year because the fairies always make a ten-year plan during those meetings and talk about how best to protect, guide, and help children of the world.

So Leezeek was not around when Queen Annabella and her guards disappeared.

King Prempper Antonio hired a countless number of investigators and used many private detectives including the city's police force without any results.

Queen Annabella and her guards, Mr. Malcolm the driver, Mr. Witherspoon the senior guard, and his assistant Mr. Rodriquez have vanished through thin air which was very strange.

King P. Antonio was very sad and frustrated with the entire situation. There was a law in the city that no king should live alone for more than six months after losing a spouse, so the king was forced to marry another woman named Hazel.

Hazel has her own story to tell, she grew up with King Prempper Antonio and went to the same school with the king and the same college. Hazel who was the daughter of the speaker of the palace grew up without her mother and that made Hazel very deceitful and bitter.

She has been in love with the king all her life without the king knowing. It was a dream come true for Hazel when she finally became King P. Antonio's wife. And so, as time went on Queen Annabella became a fading memory for the people of Apowaaii. Nevertheless, the real character of Queen Hazel came to play during the ceremony and a few days into the marriage.

This was what happened, it was the law of the land that before the ceremony the king gives the brideto-be enough money to buy gifts for the children who will attend the ceremony. Gifts like bracelets, toys, necklaces, shirts, shoes, dresses, or story books. So, anticipation and excitement were always high on the part of the children during ceremonies like the king's marriage ceremony.

Both the children and their parents alike have high hopes for the ceremony.

King Prempper Antonio being kind and caring was more than generous to the bride-to-be. However, after Hazel got the huge money for the children's gifts she went and bought green bananas, the cheapest fruit in the city, and hid them in drums and kept ninety-five percent of the money for herself. After the marriage ceremony, when it came to the time to give gifts to the children who attended the ceremony, Queen Hazel ordered the palace guards to bring two barrels covered with silky purplish gold material to the front, open it, and give one to each child at the reception.

All the guests held their breath because they thought this will be the gift of the century. Imagine their surprise of shame, when the guard started giving out a finger of green banana to each child at the reception. The cheapest gift ever given to a child at a royal ceremony in the land.

But since the children were well trained to respect and honor authority, they took the green banana graciously even though in their hearts they were disgusted and disappointed. Princess Elianna and her father, King Prempper Antonio were very hurt that Queen Hazel had disgraced and tarnished the name of the thrown by treating the precious children of Apowaaii the way she did. After the unique and creative decorations, the delicious feast, the spectacular music, and the fantastic dance only the green banana gift was the talk of the city for years.

As soon as Queen Hazel came to the palace, all the joy and the enthusiasm of the staff disappeared because Queen Hazel was authoritative, greedy, rude, and spoke to the staff of the palace like they were worthless. In a nutshell, work at the palace became stressfully hard and demanding but life goes on, the staff of the palace did their utmost best to please Queen Hazel every day and were ready every moment to answer her calls.

So, life at the palace was never the same but Princess Elianna adapted to the situation and made good use of her time by studying all kinds of subjects, science, history, mathematics, geography, sociology, and languages.

She occupied her time with studies but never forgot her exercise routine in the multi-flower garden every day. As time went on, Princess Elianna was confident and knowledgeable enough to open her own literacy program for children and adults on the east side of the palace. It became a safe haven for after-school programs also. This successful program went on for many years and the city of Apowaaii was proud of her daughter Princess Elianna.

SCIENCE
SCIENCE
HISTEMATICS
SOCOGALOGY
SOOGALOGY
LANGUAGES

Whilst all these great things were going on, people began to complain about missing precious stones, gold, and money which was very strange because nothing like this had ever happened in the city of Apowaaii. So Princess Elianna added the concerns of the people of Apowaaii to her prayer list, and every night she will pray this prayer.

"Lord God of everything, watch over me, my family and friends, and the entire world as we go to sleep until the rising bright sun wakes us up peacefully and I also ask that you give us answers to the strange things that are happening in our land this I ask in the name of your son Jesus Christ. Amen."

And every morning she will pray a similar prayer when she wakes up.

"Lord God of everything, thank you so much for breathing life into us again this morning, help us to love one another and give peace a chance as we go through the day, this I ask in the name of your son Jesus Christ. Amen."

So one day Princess Elianna had a vision in the form of a dream. And this was what she saw: She saw that in the middle of the night, Queen Hazel had been awakened by a strange noise and before she left the bed she blew an air into the nose of the king to put him to a deep sleep.

She left the room and walked to the palace meeting room which was more than a block from where the bedroom was and went straight to the huge pouch, stood there for a few minutes, and opened her mouth to the air and a brownish sand-like substance went through her mouth and nose for about five seconds.

She closed her mouth and before she could go back to the meeting room all the green bananas she gave to the children as gifts had come alive and changed into huge cream-colored centipedes with bulging dark red eyes with oval mouths. The centipedes had two long antennas just above their bulging dark red eyes as listening and communication devices.

In her vision, princess Elianna saw that there was a meeting and the centipedes were arguing among themselves. Some were saying we cannot do this anymore; this was not right against the queen and others were saying we love this we can do this for you forever in support of Queen Hazel.

Then Queen Hazel started to speak and the whole room went silent and this was what she said:

"If you disobey my command, you will be put to death by fire, you and your family. So as long as I am in charge here no more complaints. Do what you are told and live or refuse and die."

After she said that, the centipedes began to give her all the things that they had taken from people during that week. Gold bracelets, diamond rings, and lots of money. Queen Hazel took all, wrapped it in a big scarf, and breathed a greenish brown air on all the centipedes and they disappeared. Queen Hazel took the scarf filled with wealth back to her hiding place in her shoe closet and went back to bed.

In the vision princess Elianna was very frightened as she witnessed all that was going on. She awoke suddenly in a panic, her heart racing, her hands shaking, and her clothes was soaked with sweat. She quickly wrote everything in her diary, changed her clothes, and went back to sleep with these words, Lord help me, Lord help me, Lord help me as she slipped back to sleep.

Early morning Princess Elianna woke up, had her usual morning prayer, and went about her normal business like nothing ever happened. Even though she kept praying silently in her heart and mind for directions to deal with what she saw in her vision. Months went by and the disappearance of wealth from individuals in the city of Apowaaii continued without any break whatsoever until one faithful night when princess Elianna had another vision in her dream again.

This time she dreamt that she had traveled to a strange land. In that land all the people both men and women never grew old except for the texture of their hair. Some have weaved gray hair, others have straight thin gray hair, and the rest have short curls of gray hair. The hair is so beautiful and very shiny and looks like they just from a professional salon, every string was where it should be and even when the wind blew it did not affect the hair style which was very strange.

Before Princess Elianna could say a word, a beautiful well-designed chair came for her to sit and a long dining table well decorated with multishimmering colors of velvet material appeared in front of her. On the table were all types and kinds of fruits and real cooked food.

Suddenly a man and a woman came to sit at her table. The man at her left and the woman at her right side and their mouth said together these words "eat princess eat".

She replied, "Am not hungry thanks."

But they insisted that she eat because this was the food of knowledge, strength, and power and it will also open her spiritual eye to see things that the physical eye cannot see. The two fairies were her fairy grandparents and the place was a fairyland.

She became interestedly curious and decided to eat a half teaspoonful of as many kinds of food and fruits as her stomach could hold. After tasting almost half of all the things on the table she became so full that she could not breathe but her fairy grandmother told her to close her eyes, put her left hand on her heart area, and blink three times.

As soon as princess Elianna did that, she felt better than ever. She opened her eyes and looked at her left side of the table and saw that the dining table had expanded so long that she could not see the end of the table and so was her right side. And all the fairies were sitting at the dinner table with different colored wristbands.

Furthermore, their feet were not touching the ground but they were suspended in the air sitting safely about a hundred and twenty-five feet above the ground. After the feast, her fairy grandparents took her to the magic orchard where the trees grow both solid fruit and liquid fruit-like substances in a beautifully designed pot at the same time.

"This is cool grandma," said Princess Elianna.

"Whatever your hearts long for comes to be for you at that moment," replied fairy Grandma.

"So can I get real chocolate and chocolate syrup tree here?"

Before Princess Elianna could finish her sentence, the tree appeared with real chocolate hanging all over and chocolate syrup-designed pots in between the leaves.

"This is unbelievable!" said princess Elianna.

"No, like I said anything your heart desires comes to be in fairyland that was how it been and will always be," fairy Grandma.

"Wow! Good for you fairy grandma, good for you."

Her fairy grandma smiled and winked as a sign of gladness.

"Now, the instructions on how you can conquer the centipedes have been written on the paper for your eyes only, follow the instructions thoroughly and it will bring you great success. But as for your stepmother Queen Hazel, she has evil and deceit in her heart, which will unravel in due time and there is nothing anyone can do about it." Said fairy Grandpa.

"How did you know that this was the answer I was looking for fairy Grandpa?" Asked Princess Elianna.

"We can read minds," answered fairy Grandpa.

"That is weird fairy Grandpa but a very important gift to have," said Princess Elianna.

"Close your eyes Princess." asked fairy Grandpa.

Princess Elianna did as she was told and when she opened her eyes, her fairy Grandpa gave her a white and black substance in a small sunflower-designed cup and ordered her to drink.

"What is that fairy grandpa?" Asked Princess Elianna.

"This is the substance of great intuition and the power to distinguish right from wrong, it will help you in critical situations in your life," stated fairy Grandpa.

"Ok fairy Grandpa thank you so much for everything," replied Princess Elianna.

"Now for the last ritual, I call for the ancestral family hug," said fairy grandpa.

Suddenly, all the fairies with the burgundy-colored wristband came to give her a group hug. Some were as little as a fly.

Princess Elianna asked her fairy Grandpa why some fairies are as little as a fly.

Her fairy grandpa answered, "Every retired fairy is over four centuries old, and after five centuries, we become the size of a fly forever."

Fairy Grandpa stretched his right hand to touch Princess Elianna's eyes and she woke up in her bed.

"What a weird yet beautiful and helpful dream," said princess Elianna as she stretched in her bed.

She said her morning prayers: "Lord God of everything, thank you so much for breathing life into us again this morning. Help us to love one another and give peace a chance as we go through the day, this I ask in the name of your son Jesus Christ, Amen."

Princess Elianna went on with her day as she meticulously planned the destruction of the centipedes in her heart and mind.

The following day, Princess Elianna included her class and gave them the following assignment.

"Hello everyone! This is a special assignment for the class," said Princess Elianna.

"Each of you should make a pair of shoe pads in your size. On one side should be a soft cloth folded in three, glued together and the other side should be filled with sharp small rocks glued on the pad. At each end there should be a foot-long string, the two front strings will crisscross to your ankle and the two back strings will crisscross to below your knee. You have one week to complete the assignment and bring it to me for inspection." said Princess Elianna.

They all agreed and were very excited about the project. A week later they brought the shoe pads as directed and it was exactly as princess Elianna expected.

Whilst, she was in bed wrestling in her mind about how she would get the rest of the things on the list three days after the successful shoe pad project, Leezeek appeared at her window.

"Oh Princess, Princess," called Leezeek.

"Oh my God! You are here, you came at the right time. I need you more than ever." Princess Elianna said.

"Slow down princess, I knew everything, as soon as I entered your territory. Tonight, we will fly to the waterfall and get the water as needed and cross your border to the next city to get the black sand." Leezeek said.

"How did you know?" asked princess Elianna

"Princess, do you remember what I told you the first time we met? I told you I was sent by your fairy mother and I am here to help and serve you if you let me. I have a great surprise for you, your father, and all the staff in the palace but that will be revealed in due time. Right now, let us concentrate on completing the issue at hand." Leezeek stated.

So, in the deep night, Leezeek flew princess Elianna to the waterfall to get the water and flew to the next city to get the black sand. They got enough to do the job as directed.

The next day, princess Elianna told all her students about what was about to happen and when to come to the palace to wait in the classroom. Since all the students were under age princess Elianna made sure their parents had given their concert to sleep over.

Most of the children were very excited about the adventure but few were very concerned and scared. Princess Elianna called those few students and spoke to them by explaining why and how the mission was going to be completed safely and they too joined the group willingly.

On the night of the adventure, all the students were gathered in the classroom on time as ordered with their shoe pads closely by their sides. Princess Elianna gave each of the students a handkerchief and said "Keep this safe, it may come in handy."

At the stroke of midnight, as the cuckoo clock started to make noise all the students jumped up and started to make a lot of noise.

"Shhhhh," said Princess Elianna, "Remember we do not want to wake the entire people of the city or the palace. This was a secret mission and as such, we should be as quiet as the moon and the stars alright?"

And the students with lots of hidden excitement whispered "Ok Princess".

They immediately formed five groups, each group had eight students and adhered to the following instructions from princess Elianna.

"This was what we are going to do, group one you will guard the front door, group two will guard the back door, and group three will be our backup a few yards away. Groups four and five will come with me to the room to start crushing the centipedes when I say "now"." Princess Elianna explained.

"Meanwhile, everyone put your shoe pad on and secure it safely as you were taught," said Princess Elianna, and the students did exactly as they were told.

"Everyone listen up," said Princess Elianna "First, I will sprinkle the special water on the centipedes to make them very dazed and slow in movement. Then we will step on them with our stone pad shoes as quickly and strongly as we can to crush them." Explained Princess Elianna.

The leaders of the class Christopher and Vanessa asked Group one, two, and three "Are you ready?"

They replied, "Ready!"

They asked again groups four and five "Are you ready?" They also replied with a strong voice "Ready!"

"Let's do this!" And before they could finish the sentence, groups four and five busted into the classroom, and Princess Elianna quickly sprinkled the water on the centipedes, and those that were touched by the water could not move any further.

The students stepped on them, crushing them as quickly as they can, and as they were doing that, the surprised and stunned Queen Hazel blew some air from her mouth and nose on the rest of the centipedes before she disappeared.

Those that were affected grew bigger and longer and crawled faster all over the walls, the doors, and everything in the room.

"They are growing! They are growing!" Yelled Eric, Daniel and Ephraim, the three musketeers that do everything together.

Princess Elianna quickly opened the bag of black sand and called everyone to dig in and throw it over the centipedes. It became a little chaotic, some ran back and forth for the black sand because they felt like the handkerchief was too beautiful to be stained with the black sand but others opened their handkerchief, filled it with the black sand, and went to work by throwing more black sand on the centipedes.

When it was all over the rest of the centipede were burned to crisp. The students began jubilating and jumping with joy because their first adventure was a total success.

"Hello everyone, thank you so much for your help," said Princess Elianna "But, now we need to clean up like nothing ever happened. Remember, this was a secret adventure and as such should be kept secret."

The shoe pads were collected and kept in a wooden box for safekeeping. The classroom was squeaky cleaned and everything was put back in place.

"And now the main event," said Princess Elianna, "Boys on my left, girls on my right and I need volunteers."

They all raise their hands and Princess Elianna says, "Ok follow me".

They went to a couple of classrooms down the hall and saw a lot of sleeping bags and snacks.

"Take a sleeping bag and as many snacks as your hand can hold," said Princess Elianna.

The students did and that night became a slumber party sleepover. The most memorable night of their lives.

Early morning everyone went home with their sleeping bag and snacks that lasted a whole month. But as for the secret adventure, no one spoke of it ever.

Two weeks before Princess Elianna's thirteenth birthday, Queen Hazel's greediness and her deceitful heart emerged and she colluded with three gangsters from another city to come through the private tunnels known and used only by the royal family to the palace.

Queen Hazel and the gangsters went into the crown room and stole all the crowns of the throne. Some crowns were made of pure gold, others were made of different kinds of diamonds, crystals, and expensive pearls. The crowns have been in the family for generations and were priceless in value.

Queen Hazel and her gangsters kept all the crowns in a huge thirty-gallon plastic bag, dug a big hole under the biggest tree in the left corner of the land, put the plastic bag full of priceless crowns in the hole, and buried it.

With the view that in a few months when the dust is settled, they will dig it up and go and sell it to the highest bidder.

After that Queen Hazel started acting suspiciously by asking the staff often "Is everything alright around here?" which was odd because first of all, she had never asked anyone in the palace how they were doing ever. Secondly, she does not care about anyone but herself which makes that question sound awkward, bizarre, and suspicious.

Life in the city of Apowaaii began to return to normal because the citizens stopped complaining about missing money, gold, and precious stones. Princess Elianna continued her studies and her social work and whenever she needed anything her father the King was there to help her get it, or get through whatever situation she encountered.

When Princess Elianna had her period at age thirteen, Miss Hanson the cook helped her learn how she can manage her daily dressing during those days since she is not close to her stepmother as she needed to be.

So as hours turned to days and days turned to weeks and weeks turned to months, Princess Elianna did all she could to return to normalcy. She planned a dinner party with the help of her father King Antonio for all the children in the city of Apowaaii a few weeks after her thirteenth birthday.

It was huge and memorable. The food preparation took over a week because of the number of children that attended the party. The king hired the police band to play for the children during the dinner party and it was spectacular. For the party gifts, the boys had silver-plated watches and the girls had crystal earrings and necklaces. The children had the time of their lives, even those who could not attend had their share of the food and the gift sent to their various homes through the friends that came. That party was one for the record books and was talked about for generations.

After the party princess Elianna had a big surprise, her cousin Serene, a superstar musician who happens to be a British-born citizen came to visit for a few hours. After a lengthy conversation, cousin Serene sang the most beautiful birthday song princess Elianna has ever heard. Even though it was one piano, it sounded like a whole orchestra was performing at that moment. It was absolutely mesmerizing.

Princess Elianna took her cousin to the crown room to show her all the crowns from her ancestor's time to date. That was when princess Elianna discovered that all the crowns were gone.

"The crowns are gone, the crowns are gone! oh my God! How can this happen," Princess Elianna cried loudly in the crown's room. Her cousin Serene tried her best to console her but to no avail.

"First, my mother disappeared, and now the crowns? What next? This is too much for one person to take," said Princess Elianna, but cousin Serene continually consoled her until sudden calmness came upon her.

"Anyway, these are all vanities, I am just going to concentrate on what lies ahead of me and the city," said Princess Elianna.

Princess Elianna has seen Leezeek in the crown's room window during her cry and that gave her a sense of calmness. She realized that Leezeek could help her find the robbers who came and took the entire crowns without the guards or the staff seeing them.

"The robbers will be dealt with swiftly as the law demands when they are cut," stated Princess Elianna to cousin Serene.

"I am very sorry cousin Serene, that, I could not show you all the beautiful crowns of this thrown, something that we have communicated about several times over the years. I hope to God the next time you visit it will be a successful crown story," said Princess Elianna.

"I hope so too," answered Cousin Serene.

Early morning the king's secretary took Serene to the airport to catch a flight to London where she lives with her parents. The news of the stolen royal crowns got to King Prempper and he told the guards and the entire staff to keep an eye out for the crowns as the police investigate.

At midnight, Leezeek came to princess Elianna and told her the greatest news ever.

"First good news, I know who took your crowns, and second good news, your mother is still alive but trapped in the underworld," said Leezeek.

"I know how to get her back."

"Hallelujah! Hallelujah! Hallelujah!" Exclaimed Princess Elianna.

"Oh yes! God is great all the time." "So are you saying for sure my mother is alive and well and that you can bring her back to me right here in this palace again?"

"Please be calm, the answer is yes to all your questions." Leezeek said.

"Wait, how about her driver and her two guards," asked Princess Elianna.

"They are all well, however, I will need help from your little soldiers." Asked Leezeek.

"I do not have little soldiers," answered princess Elianna.

"I mean your students," explained Leezeek.

"Oh! Ok, tell me what to do," answered princess Elianna.

"You know, I am going to tell you the history of your land before we plan the rescue mission," said Leezeek.

"Yes! I love history it makes you compare how much things have evolved," answered Princess Elianna.

"Long time ago, before your ancestors took over this land there were your original first settlers in the land. They were very beautiful both inside and out. They were kind, caring, and possessed magic powers but they had two major problems."

"First, they grew in height to only two and a half feet no matter how long they exercised and ate the right food. Two, they grew extra ears on their forehead by age seventeen both girls and boys."

"In the beginning, they decided to cut it off but they found out that the more the extra ear on the forehead was cut off the bigger it grew back with accelerated speed. They were also very good at good magic spells but the more they tried to eliminate the third ear on their forehead with different magic spells, the worse the ear became. No amount of magic could change their appearance for a very long time." Leezeek continues.

"However, as time went on, the women started giving birth to little giants. Children who grew taller up to five feet and did not grow a third ear on the forehead by age seventeen, but they too fell short of possessing the ability to do magic and had no patience to give peace a chance during arguments. The giants began to call the old people dwarfs in a funny way. Nevertheless, the dwarfs were overwhelmed with love and joy that their generation had changed the trajectory of the human race."

"The dwarfs decided to leave to the underworld but swore that every century they would return to check the land and see the type of change and progress their descendants have acquired. It just happened that the very day the dwarfs were inspecting the land between 12 am and 3 am was the same time Queen Annabella and her guards were traveling back home from the medical conference. They were accidentally taken by the dwarfs during their magic spell to the underworld and since then the queen and her guards have tried several times to get out of the underworld back to their families but to no avail. They are there as quests, not in any danger, not in prison, and not being used as servants. In fact, Queen Annabella and her guards were made leaders by the elders of dwarf land because of their height and their beautiful figures." Iterated by Leezeek.

After the long talk, Leezeek saw that princess Elianna had fallen asleep so he left till the next night.

"As I said last night, Queen Annabella and her guards are being treated with respect and honor and there was no cause for concern about their health and treatments," said Leezeek respectfully.

"There was one hurdle though, the gate to dwarf land cannot be opened until the next inspection time which is ninety-seven years from now that is why we have to find our way to them." Leezeek said.

"Ok Leezeek, so what now?" Princess Elianna asked.

"We have to go to the magic forest, between midnight and 3 am and find the second gate to dwarf land in the underworld. The second gate was installed many years ago by the fairies to get to children of dwarf land to help them through their personality crises. And also, to help them understand, accept, and be proud of who they were. Because sometimes being different is a great thing," said Leezeek.

"This is why I need your student's help because the magic forest is huge and we need as many people as we can to search for the second gate." Leezeek continued.

"But can't you use your magic powers to find it yourself?" Asked Princess Elianna.

"No princess, I cannot because it was installed by the fairies, so this is above my pay grade, anything done by the fairies I cannot penetrate."

"Wow, so you work under the fairies then, is that right?" Princess Elianna asked.

"Yes, princess you are exactly right," Leezeek answered.

"First, get permission for the weekend from all your students' parents, and inform the students about the gathering at your multi-purpose guest room before midnight. At midnight, I will come and blow fairy spells on all the students and as we fly so will all the children be able to fly to the magic forest. In the forest, the only job of the students will be to touch each tree with their palms and listen to the response of the tree. The trees in the magic forest have their own personalities and as such will give each student a statement or a question when touched." Leezek explained.

"This sounds a little weird but whatever it takes to bring my mother back to me I am all for it," added Princess Elianna.

"Do not forget to keep the windows open," asked Leezeek.

"Ok," replied princess Elianna.

So princess Elianna did as Leezeek asked and got permission for the entire weekend from all the forty student's parents and they gathered in the multipurpose guest room and kept the window open.

By midnight as all the students fell asleep, Leezeek came and performed a fairy spell on all the students by sprinkling rainbow crystals in the air in the room with these words:

"Even though all of you will fly to the magic forest, only a few with brave heart will use your palms to touch as many trees as you can until we find the second gate. By touching the tree, the tree will come alive, reveal its personality, and give you important information. Sometimes the information will be unbelievably annoying or hurtful or funny. Through this magic spell, you will possess a mature open mind to engage and argue your point from your heart, mind, and soul for a few minutes at a time. When is all over after the second gate is found, and our mission is accomplished, you will fly back with me to this very room safely but you will never remember anything about the magic forest, how you got there, or the argument you had with the magic trees."

As soon as Leezeek said those words the students started flying one by one through the window and when they got to the magic forest, Esperanza touched a tree with her palm, it was the tree of disrespect because the tree said, "What a hell do you want from me?" Esperanza responded "Sorry not you," and went to the next tree.

Joel touched The Tree of Laughter and the tree started laughing so hard it echoed the whole forest which made all the other students laugh from afar, Joel also started laughing so hard his eyes started tearing, and he said thanks for making me laugh and moved on.

Kwame touched The Tree of Business and the tree said "Hi, would you like to learn how to make money in business?" Kwame replied, "I wish I had enough time but is there any way you can sum it all up in a few words?" Asked Kwame.

"Oh yeah," said The Tree of Business.

"For a good business to flourish and make money, you must have a great business plan, qualified employees, and a good location, location, location." Tree of Business uttered.

"Thank you, Tree of Business," and Kwame moved on to the next tree.

Vera touched The Tree of Kindness and the tree said "Hello, would you like to sit down?" Vera answered "I wish I could but, time is of the essence to me right now so no, thank you anyway," and moved on to the next tree.

Maxwell touched The Tree of Superiority and the tree said, "How dare, you touch me with your filthy small hands." Maxwell replied "My hands are as clean as a whistle and just so you know my hands are normal size for my age, but I apologize for disturbing you," and he moved on to the next tree.

The Tree of Emotions was touched by James and this is the statement the Tree made. "Hi, am always happy when people are happy but my happiness is short-lived because of physical pain when people are sick with incurable diseases, when innocent souls are being lost through mass shootings in schools, in entertainment settings, in communities, and in wars. Am emotionally drained for love once, families, and friends who are always in mourning. Am also in great emotional pain when some communities have beautiful housing inside and out, better schools with all needed supplies, well-paid teachers, and clean communities with no liquor stores within the vicinity but other communities have the total opposite of every good thing a community should have including multiple liquor stores in every block of the street. I cannot comprehend when some people are given less punishment but others are given outrageous insane punishments for the same crimes. Am always in emotional distress for what has happened, what is happening, and what is about to happen. This makes my life a living mess all the time." Tree of Emotions stated.

"I am very, very sorry for what you are going through. I wish I had the power to take some of your pain away," said James sorrowfully.

"However, this is what I can do, I will continue to pray to God on your behalf to give you the strength to endure your emotions always," added James.

"Thank you so much!" said The Tree of Emotions, and James moved on to the next tree.

Richie touched The Tree of Bullying and this is what the tree said. "Hey! Did you bring your lunch money like I ordered you to Moon Face? If not, I will call my friends and together we will beat you up again."

"No! I did not bring any lunch money and you and your friends dare not touch me, because I will report you to Mr. Goodman the principal and you and your friends will be expelled from the school according to the new bullying reg- ulation." Said Richie forcefully, and The Tree of Bullying be- came quiet and scared. And Richie boldly moved on to the next tree.

Tree of Health was touched by Anastasia and the tree said "Hi, am going to give you a few tips to living a very healthy life."

"Ok," said Anastasia.

"Always wash your hands with soap and water before you touch your food and after you finish playing with your friends or your toys. Choose water over all other sweet sub- stances, eat breakfast every day, and do not forget to drink your milk. Eat your fruits and vegetables and always ask for protein with meals. Brush your teeth twice a day and rinse your mouth in between brushing. Exercise half an hour three to four times a week or be active every day. Take showers as often as you can, get enough rest, do not talk to strangers and if you are ever confused about anything at all, do not hesitate to ask a grownup for answers. Know that there is always an answer to a question or a puzzle, and that help is available for those that seek it." Add The Tree of Health.

"Thanks a lot," said Anastasia and she moved on to the next tree.

The tree of Religion was touched by Joshua and the tree said "Bless you, my child. Would you like to hear about the Supreme Commander of all things?"

"Do you mean the president?" Asked Joshua.

"No! Am talking about God," said The Tree of Religion.

"Oh! I love to," said Joshua. "I always have time for God and his words because according to my parents, due to medical circumstances when I was born, I did not breathe for a few minutes and the doctors and nurses kept on working on me to revive me."

"But my parents prayed their hearts out to God and He listened and blew life into me again and I started breathing. From that moment onward, God became the center of our family. So, wherever I go, I always show care and kindness to people around me the same way God showed kindness to me by giving me life. So as I said, I always have time for God. As for me, all the laws in the Bible can be summed up to this statement "Love your neighbor as yourself "." Joshua added.

"Wow! My child, I could not have said it any better. Thank you and be blessed always," said The Tree of Religion.

Josephine touched a tree and it was The Tree of Harmony. The tree said, "Hello, I am going to give you just a tip to help you in life. Always say please when is appropriate and do not feel too big to say I am sorry when you are wrong or to agree to disagree. Always resolve misunderstands before sundown. Remember to treat people the way you would like to be treated and say thank you for the little gestures in life. Never cease to say I love you to your love once in times of confusion for tomorrow is overrated. Furthermore, in everything be patient and give peace a chance no matter what. If and when you follow these rules to the best of your knowledge, life will be gracious to you always." Add The Tree of Harmony.

"Thanks a lot," said Josephine and she moved on to the next tree.

Charles touched a tree and it was the Tree of Silence because no reaction from the tree for a full minute. As Charles was leaving, the tree said, "Sometimes it's better to keep silent and reflect on the past, the present, and wonder about the future." Charles said "Thanks" and moved on to the next tree.

The tree of Gossip was touched by KK. And the tree said, "Hi, would you like to hear juicy details of a famous man?"

"Who?" Said KK.

"I want you to guess," said the Tree of Gossip.

"Once upon a time, a boy was born to a couple who were all immigrants. A mother from Scotland and a father from Germany. The couple were blessed with beautiful children but during that time racism, segregation, and male power were the dominant wind that was blowing over the most compassionate, kind, and caring Country that they lived in."

"So at the dinner table, those were the discussions that went on as the children were going up, the same discussions happened in schools, communities, and around playgrounds. The children became successful and one of them followed his father's footsteps and became famous in real estate just like his father was. Along the way, this famous man became the most cunning and deceitful person of his time. In a nutshell, he became the greatest con artist in the world."

"Really?" Asked KK.

"Yes! He was able to deceive contractors who supplied him with things, deceive workers who worked for him by filing multiple bankruptcies to raid them of their retirement benefits and open a fake school to extract money from venerable people who were looking to start businesses in real estate just to name a few. The greatest con was when he was able to talk himself out of sexual misconduct allegations, even when there was enough evidence to support almost a dozen women's allegations of sexual misconduct." Said The Tree of Gossip.

"Furthermore, this famous con man was able to step on all norms, bully his opponents during campaigns, brainwash part of the Country with his dog whistle, race-baiting, inhumane, draconian statements, and sort collisional help to become the leader of the free world." The tree of Gossip continues.

"Wow! What a shocker!" Said KK.

"Yes! The story does not end here, but I will leave you with this for now until we meet again," said The Tree of Gossip.

"Right, thank you Tree of Gossip," and KK shaking his head moved on to the next tree.

"The Tree of the Future was touched by Theresa and Agatha, the tree said, "Do you know whom or what humanity's greatest enemy is?" Theresa and Agatha said, "maybe not doing the right thing?"

And the tree said, "You are half right. The greatest enemy of human beings is themselves, their anger, their disrespect for each other, and their disrespect for the environment. Until we all have a leveled plain field in everything, and I mean everything, our future will be as shady and scary as a mob boss's contract."

"So how do we change that?" Asked Theresa.

"Good question," answered The Tree of the Future. "First, we need to treat the environment with real respect and leave it better than we found it, or else it will destroy us in a split second. Also, we should learn to treat each other with respect and dignity because when people feel and think that they have been treated unfairly multiple times, that is when the seed of dislike is sown and as time goes on it geminate and bear fruit to hatred. And hatred has so many dangerous and manipulating branches that, if not cut from the root immediately, and the area burnt to ashes, re-cement, and beautiful lovely scented flowers decorated in that area literally, an entire generation will have to endure the consequences of that single dislike seed that has germinated into a full-blown hatred fruit. And like I said, a leveled plain field in everything especially our justice system will be a good start"

"Wow, this is mind bordering," added Agatha.

"Furthermore, "charity begins at home but does not end there"." Add the tree of the Future, "Let us start in our individual homes by training our children the way we want them to be treated, practice respect and responsibility, give relentless explanations about cause and effect, and the rest will fall into its rightful place."

"Wow, that is a lot to think about," said Theresa, "Thank you Tree of the Future." And they moved on to the next tree with the message engraved in their hearts.

Emmanuel touched a tree and it was The Tree of Presidents and the tree said, "Do you know the names of all the presidents and the time they ruled?"

"No, I only know a few of them, sir," said Emmanuel.

"Ok then, since you are pressed for time, I will give you the names of the first seven and the last sixteenth presidents, the rest you can find out in the history books in your own time," said the tree of presidents.

"Ok sir," said Emmanuel, and the tree said the

following:

Name of President	Date of Birth	Time ruled	Number
George Washington	2/22/1732	1789-1797	1st
John Adams	10/30/1735	1797-1801	2nd
Thomas Jefferson	4/13/1743	1801-1809	3rd
James Madison	3/16/1751	1809-1817	4th
James Monroe	4/28/1758	1817-1825	5th
John Quincy Adams	7/11/1767	1825-1829	6th
Andrew Jackson	3/15/1767	1829-1837	7th
Herbert Hoover	8/10/1874	1929-1933	30th
Franklin D. Roosevelt	1/30/1882	1933-1945	31st
Harry S. Truman	5/8/1884	1945-1953	32nd
Dwight D. Eisenhower	10/14/1890	1953-1961	33rd
John F. Kennedy	5/29/1917	1961-1963	34th
Lyndon B. Johnson	8/27/1908	1963-1969	35th
Nixon Richard	1/9/1913	1969-1974	36st
Gerald Ford	7/14/1913	1974-1977	37th
Jimmy Carter Jr.	10/1/1924	1977-1981	38th
Ronald Reagan	2/6/1911	1981-1989	39th
George H.W. Bush	6/12/1924	1989-1993	40th
Bill Clinton	8/19/1946	1993-2001	41st
George W. Bush	7/6/1946	2001-2009	42nd
Barack Obama	8/4/1961	2009-2017	43rd
Donald Trump	6/14/1946	2017-2021	44th
Joe Biden	11/20/1947	2021-2025	45th

"Wow! Thank you, Tree of Presidents. This is the greatest information anyone has ever given me," said Emmanuel and he moved on to the next tree.

Ernest and Joanne touched a tree and it was The Tree of Journalism and the tree said, "For centuries I have been the true source of information for the entire world. My family and I have worked so hard to report all sorts of news, some great, others not so great, but always made sure that we are reporting the truth of whatever is happening. The world loves us with its heart and soul and believes us with its engaged mind. However, for a few years now and for some unknown reason, few people and their gangsters are trying to destroy our reputation and our integrity by saying as many times as they can and any chance, they get that we deliver fake news. Also calling my family members who are great journalist's enemies of the state which is a very dangerous statement to make."

"Meanwhile, the leader of the gang is a con man who can spin any news to his advantage. I am saddened by these outbursts but that will never detour my family and I from working very hard to bring the real true information that can be verified by intelligent and smart people around the world. I pray that journalism will remain a transparent, truthful, and highly recommended carrier for generations to come." Add the tree of journalism.

"Thank you so very much," said Ernest and Joanne and they moved on to the next tree.

This went on for hours with every student trying very hard to find the second gate till Athena touched The Tree of Memory and the tree said, "Hello would you like me to remember something for you?"

Athena replied, "Yes! When was the last time the gate of Dwarf land opened?"

"About three years ago," the tree answered.

"Can you tell me where to find the second gate?" Athena asked.

"No!!! Am not allowed to talk about the second gate to anyone," answered The Tree of Memory.

"Please just this once for it is very important." Athena pleaded with The Tree of Memory.

"Ok! Just this once, go straight from here count to the sixty-seventh tree, and turn right there is a big tree surrounded by small short trees, the gate is under one of the short trees."

"Thank you so much Tree of Memory I will forever be grateful," said Athena.

"Hello everyone, I think I've found it," and everyone began to run toward Athena's way.

Meanwhile, Leezeek and princess Elianna have sported what seems like the gate in the middle of the forest from the clouds and were flying down to the area. Together all met at where The Tree of Memory directed Athena. Leezeek blew special wind at the area and the second gate emerged.

The gate was opened and it was a tunnel. On both sides were huge candles on beautiful golden stands and in each corner were multicolored huge stunning candles. Each student was ordered to take one and light it, they did and the entire tunnel came alive with beautiful pictures of the moon, the sun, and the stars painted in unique oils on the wall of the tunnel.

There were no stairs, but as they walked, it felt like they were going downstairs and everyone's memory card activated. Each of them began to see the very moment they were born and every minute thereafter. It was mesmerizing and they were all cut in the moment in time.

By the time they realized they had walked more than an hour to a black and white dotted and heart-shaped curtain, they opened it and saw the most spectacular city they had ever seen. The entire city was built with velvet and burgundy crystals crafted within a gigantic waterfall. However, when you go through the waterfall you do not get wet and the waterfall is only seen when you are outside the city.

Before they can ask a question, they were met with a lot of the dwarfs and they begin to treat them like royalty. The dwarfs took them to a big dining room and they were given different kinds of delicious substances that filled them like food. As they were busy talking about the city and the drinks, Queen Annabella appeared to them. The students with great excitement and happiness jumped up and down with screams but Princess Elianna was shocked to see her mother pretty as ever and was not able to move from her seat.

Her mother hurriedly came to her with open arms and gave her the longest hug and kisses ever and said "Yes! Elianna it's me."

As all these were happening, the dwarfs were very happy that the queen was finally rescued.

However, in the middle of the celebration one of the dwarfs suddenly asked, "How did these children get here? Did anyone open the gate before time?"

Before anyone could answer, Leezeek appeared blew a strong air over the entire place, everyone became still except all the dwarfs. Leezeek explained the mission to the dwarfs and the dwarfs were appreciative and cooperative of Leezeek and the children. By the time everyone came too, the three guards were sitting among them, and the gathering became a send-off party for Queen Annabella and her guards.

The party continued for hours until at the stroke of midnight, the elders of dwarf land with the help of Leezeek worked magic that took the Queen, the guards, Princess Elianna, and the students back to the magic forest.

As they were flying to their final destination from the magic forest, Leezeek and Princess Elianna had the perfect plan to hide Queen Annabella and her guards until the king's fiftieth birthday party celebration which was less than a week away.

"That will be my perfect gift for my father and the greatest news for the citizens of the city of Apowaaii," said Princess Elianna.

"Oh yes, and do not forget this will be the perfect chance to tell your people what Queen Hazel has done." Add Leezeek.

When they got to the multipurpose room the students fell in deep sleep until the following day. No one remembered anything about the magic forest or dwarf land or the rescue mission. The students spent the rest of the weekend at the palace, camping, hiking, and swimming. King Prempper Antonio made sure the students were safe and well cared for by the staff. Never once, did Queen Hazel come to say hello to the students whilst they were staying in the palace.

The leaders of the palace did their uttermost best to plan the king's fiftieth birthday party. In fact, they all went overboard with the decorations, because they hired five party planners for the occasion, three different bands, and three more chefs including the kitchen staff. Whilst all these were going on, Princess Elianna was enjoying secret quality time with her mother Queen Annabella in part of the palace.

The palace is huge, and sits on about six football fields. Three of the fields house a hospital with staff apartments, a college and boarding area, an entertainment center, and a sports stadium with multiple parking garages.

On the day of the king's birthday party, as all the lovely citizens of Apowaaii gather at the palace royal party room and on the outside lawn, the King spoke and this is what the King Prempper Antonio said:

"My fellow citizens of Apowaaii, before we start the party I would like to ask that anyone who knows anything about the royal stolen crowns should speak out now and your punishment will be considered with leniency, if not when you are caught, you will be given the maximum punishment set by the law of the land."

The place was as quiet as a cemetery and you can hear a pin drop but no one came forward. So the pastor of the city Pastor Joe prayed and the party got started.

In the middle of the feast, as people were drinking, eating, and dancing, Leezeek used his magic powers to change into a real person, and took the microphone and this is what he said:

"May the King live forever and may the citizens of Apowaaii be blessed always. Hello, my name is Leezeek I have two great news for the King and the people of Apowaaii. First, I know those who stole the royal crowns and the place where the crowns are buried. I already have three gangsters and they will tell us who their leader is when they begin to talk."

The people started moving toward where the gangsters were, with the view of going to do them harm but the King stood up and said "Nobody move!"

Everyone stood still. "Where are the gangsters?" Asked the king.

They are all handcuffed together about one hundred yards from here." Leezeek answered.

King Prempper ordered the royal guards to go and bring the gangsters and they did as they were told. Suddenly, Queen Hazel nervously got up to walk away but the King said,

"My Queen could you give me a few more minutes, please. I would like to get to the bottom of this situation," and the queen sat back down with her entire body shaking like a dry leave.

When the gangsters came this is what they said:

"Few months ago, Queen Hazel contacted us and made a deal with us that if we agreed to steal the royal crowns and hide them and wait a few months, she would sell the crowns to the highest bidder and ten percent of the proceeds will be given to us to share."

"She also said that the crowns are wealth millions. So as planned, one night Queen Hazel led us through the royal tunnels and to the crowns room and we stole all the crowns and bagged it and buried it under the biggest tree in the left corner of the land," said one of the gangsters.

First, the citizens were shocked and damn founded then, they became angry and started cursing and booing Queen Hazel.

The gangsters took some of the royal guards to where the crowns were buried and it was retrieved, cleaned and polished, and returned to the royal family. As for Queen Hazel, she was found guilty of theft, keeping stolen property on royal grounds, and withholding information. The King stripped her of her crown and her title, and his marriage to her was instantaneously nullified. The guards were ordered to take the disgraced Hazel and her gangsters to jail for a very long time.

This situation put a damp on the party, but the King stood up and said in a strong happy voice let the party continue. The citizens of Apowaaii were not surprised but cheered because there was a rumor going on in the land that since they got married, the King had not consummated the marriage. So the music started again and the people began to act like nothing had happened. Drinking, eating, and dancing went on for hours then, Princess Elianna took the microphone and said, "Hello may I have your attention, please!"

And everything went silent, "And now, the final piece of the puzzle, first, Father I am very sorry that I have not told you what am about to say to the citizens of Apowaaii." Princess Elianna stated.

"Come on princess do not keep me in suspense, say what's on your mind already," said King Prempper Antonio. For he has taken in some drinks and feels a little tipsy.

"Father embrace yourself, my mother and her guards are alive," said Princess Elianna.

Everyone including the King yelled. "What? How can that happen?"

"Yes! Father see for yourself," added princess Elianna.

The entire group including the King turned to their left side and did not see anything so they quickly turned to their right side and there came the elegant lady of Apowaaii Queen Annabella more beautiful than ever and her guards.

The citizens of Apowaaii began screaming at the top of their lungs, some were jumping up and down, and others took the silk material decorations and laid it on the ground for her to walk on.

The King jumped up from his seat run and lifted Queen Annabella up like she weighed nothing. He then gave her the longest kiss ever and said "Welcome back my love, I will never let you out of my sites ever."

Everyone began to laugh and cry, tears of joy. As the King and the Queen began to dance the night away, the citizens of Apowaaii started asking a lot of questions. Until some were bold enough to approach princess Elianna directly.

"How did this happen?" they asked princess Elianna.

"It's a long story and I cannot tell you anything about it," said Princess Elianna.

"However, I am very grateful and thankful to the Almighty God for working such a great miracle for my family and the citizens of Apowaaii," she added.

And all the people responded "Amen".

With excitement and joyous heart, the party continued till the next day. After the party, King Prempper called Leezeek several times with the thought of giving him a generous gift for his help in solving the stolen crowns issue but Leezeek was nowhere to be found.

However, Leezeek continued his secret relationship with princess Elianna for decades as promised. King Antonio Prempper and Queen Annabella went on to have other children and they are Eliora, Riah, and Daxton.

Princess Elianna took them under her wings literally and taught them everything that she knows. And the beautiful royal family and the citizens of Apowaaii overwhelmed with love and joy lived peacefully, harmoniously, and happily ever after.

The end.